ISBN: 061576911X
ISBN-13: 9780615769110
Library of Congress Control Number: 2013902978
CreateSpace Independent Publishing Platform
North Charleston, South Carolina

To our beautiful mother, Judissa Anders, for her heart of gold
and endless wealth of love, strength, support and inspiration.

ACKNOWLEDGEMENTS

A special 'thank you' to our cousin Tom Moran for his master editing skills; to Mateo Gamlen for his heartfelt belief, continuous support and hard work with the design, layout and video; to Dugan O'Neal for his video expertise, humor and wit; to Hernan Savastano for his skills and dedication on 'setting up shop,' and to Paul Owen Lewis, Eric Watson, Bryn Barnard and Roger Fernandes for reading our story and providing wonderful reviews. To Janeen, Litonya and Crea for their love and enthusiasm, and to Lexi for striking all the right poses!

May Tani's story inspire and uplift the hearts of all who come to know her.

TANI'S SEARCH FOR THE HEART

Keith Egawa and Chenoa Egawa

In a small clearing, within the wide woods of the Pacific Northwest, sat a village. And at the outskirts of that village was a modest little house where Tani lived with her grandmother. Their home was not far from the shores of the great water known by their people as the Salish Sea, and beyond the Salish Sea was the ocean. Like the other houses of the village, Tani's was made of mismatched planks, the white paint of which had chipped and faded over the years, until the color was that of the trees surrounding the homes of her people. The shingles on the roof were almost always dark with water from the heavy rains, and moss grew on them most of the year, until the sun of summer dried out the cracks and crevices again. There were gaps in the boards of Tani's house, and in the fall wind blew through in hidden places, making whistling noises like visiting spirits. But when it was cold Tani's grandmother built a fire in their black iron stove, and stoked the coals late into the night to make sure her little granddaughter stayed warm.

Tani's grandmother taught her many things. She spoke of legends and the brave adventures of Tani's ancestors. She told stories of the Stick Indian, a magical being of wood, branches and leaves, who dwelled in the forest since long before Tani's people. She told Tani how encountering the Stick Indian could seem a frightening prospect, scratching at people's windows during the night with long twiggy fingers. But despite this, his presence in the shadows of the wilds kept children from disobeying their parents and wandering off alone, for fear of finding themselves face to face with a tree that had suddenly come to life. A tall gnarled figure with twisted, spindly limbs. And just as all creatures and spirits of the land had their place, he too was an ancient part of the forest, enduring since the world was young. He too played an important role in the cycle of the natural world.

Grandmother told Tani how people often heard the Stick Indian from far back in the trees, whistling like the high note played on a carved wooden flute, though almost no one ever saw him, unless he had a very good reason for showing himself. And of all the fantastic possibilities imparted by her grandmother's soft and steady voice, this one was Tani's favorite; even though she was not sure whether or not she believed the Stick Indian was truly real.

Before bedtime Grandmother spoke of all the animals their people shared the land with, and how each lived with an important purpose, from ants to eagles, bumblebees to bears. She knew more than the simple truths about the creatures that crawled upon the ground, flew through the air and swam in the water. She knew of an older time when the animals could do things people no longer witness. A time when animals could speak in the language of humans.

"You mean the animals used to talk with people?" Tani had asked in disbelief, as she and Grandmother sat by the stove on a cold fall night, the way they always did.

"Used to?" said Grandmother, laying a hand on top of Tani's head. "They can still speak. But only when they trust you with the strongest trust imaginable. A trust that must be earned. And only if they are certain their words will affect the way you walk upon the earth from that moment on. Then maybe, just maybe, you will hear their voices."

One evening Tani's uncle appeared unexpectedly in the doorway, on a night Tani would remember for the moon being especially bright. She could see moths flapping and darting to and fro, as the light from the moon made her uncle's shadow fall all the way across the floorboards to where she sat sewing a small pouch of deer hide. Uncle and grandmother sat down at the table where Tani and Grandmother ate their meals together, and they spoke in quiet, serious voices. Tani only caught bits and pieces of the words that passed between them, but she heard her uncle say, "They are cutting more of it down."

Upon hearing these words Grandmother fell silent. She looked over to where her granddaughter sat sewing by the fire, and for many moments she stared into Tani's eyes. Then, as Uncle was leaving, he said, "The logging trucks are coming." And when the door closed behind him Tani saw there was a great powdery moth sitting on the floor, trapped within the house. Grandmother slowly rose to her feet and walked over to where the bug awaited his fate, his wings trembling slightly. She knelt down and let the moth walk cautiously onto her extended finger. Then she held her hand before the open window where the moon shined high and bright, allowing the insect to flap back out into the night.

The next morning, while they ate their breakfast of fried potatoes and smelt, Grandmother finally spoke of the night before. "Tani," she said, "They are coming to cut down more of the trees. They will take them in trucks and on ships to cities near and far, even to places across the ocean. Like times before, they will take only some. But they will keep returning until someday it will all be gone. The world needs special people who can stand up and speak for those who will be hurt by losses such as this. Special people who will help others realize the truths of their actions. It is not only the trees I speak of, as people have always harvested from the land to better their lives. What must concern you is when men take from the world in a way where things cannot be given back or replaced. I speak of all things affected by man in this disrespectful way."

Tani nodded her head, but said nothing.

For the next four days and nights Grandmother was very quiet. But each morning she made her way out to the pebbled clearing in front of the house and sang to the rising sun. Then every evening she sang to the darkening sky. And each time, Tani stood in the doorway, or sat at the open window, listening because she loved the songs. And on the last such night, Grandmother had Tani stand by her side as she sang, leaning on her granddaughter's shoulder to help rest the stiffness in her old bones. And when the song was finished, Tani thought she heard a whistling, soft but clear, coming from deep within the great forest.

Once back inside the house, Grandmother sat Tani down at the table and took both of her granddaughter's hands in hers. "Tani, you must go into the forest," she said. "Journey to where the ocean flows into the Salish Sea. Far out to where I took you clam digging one year ago. Do you remember it?"

Tani thought this over, imagining many miles of sandy shore, and the water that seemed to have no end when she looked out toward the horizon. "All by myself?" She asked. "But I do not know if I remember the way."

"You remember enough," said Grandmother smiling. "And what you do not remember you will be shown. You will not be alone. Trust my words, as I would never send you on such a journey if I did not know this to be true."

"And why do I go?" asked Tani.

At this grandmother took Tani's round face in her two old hands, and the smile left her. "Tani, you must find the heart. The heart of the world. The heart of the people. The heart of all that lives. That is what you will find on this journey."

When the orange glow from the embers no longer shown through the slits of the stove's cast-iron door, Grandmother whispered something into the still darkness of the room. "You have been on this journey before with me. But this time you will go by a road you have never taken."

During the night Tani's grandmother passed on. And with sadness pushing away all other thoughts, Tani moved into the home of her uncle, aunt, and little cousin, Droopy Drawers, just a short walk down the narrow dirt road from where Tani had lived for many happy years. Over the next few days and nights Tani began to think about what her grandmother had said. When she cried she would see her grandmother's face, and would feel the strength in her words. Then she would fall asleep, dreaming of the great lonely woods and the endless ocean. She would hear the comforting sounds of strange but friendly voices she had never heard before, encouraging her on a long journey through places she had not yet seen in waking life.

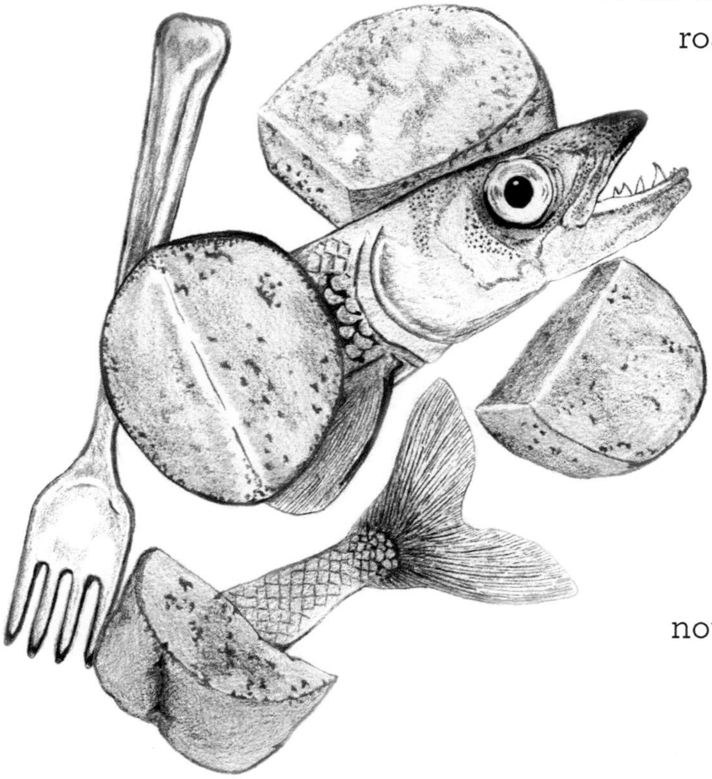

Many days passed in Tani's new home, until she had nearly forgotten her grandmother's guidance. And then one night as she played with Droopy Drawers, a large moth flapped into the open window and made several turns about the room, before flying back out into the night. Then an old voice softly spoke the words, "it is time, Dear One. It is time to travel." Tani looked around the room at the faces of her aunt and uncle. But they had not heard the soft whisper of the mysterious voice. They had not seen the moth. Only Droopy Drawers looked wide-eyed toward the open window.

The next morning Tani awoke earlier than usual. By now the deer-hide pouch she had been working on was finished, so she filled it to bulging with a mix of dried fish and berries, stowing her folding knife in her pocket. And with dew clinging to the tall stalks of grass around her uncle's house, Tani set out, heading in the direction of the ocean. The only person who witnessed her walking away from the village that morning was her little cousin Droopy Drawers, who stood silently in her sagging diaper watching this important moment; her prized red yoyo dragging behind her on the ground. Little Droopy Drawers watched her older cousin until Tani's figure disappeared down a path through the trees. Then she again turned her attention to the yoyo, thinking thoughts of breakfast and a fresh diaper.

After walking only a short distance, Tani came to a sudden stop, realizing she now stood at the farthest edge of the land she was familiar with. And for what seemed like a long and uncertain while, she stared toward the distant tops of cedar and fir trees, towering far off in the direction of the unknown. There were several paths from which Tani now had to choose, and she was doubtful as to which choice was the right one. Only weeks ago she would have simply asked her grandmother what to do. But now, out here in the wilds, she felt even sadder and more alone than on the day of her grandmother's departure from this world. So she furrowed her brow and struggled to find strength. And as she remembered the certainty in her grandmother's words when she spoke of the important task at hand, there was suddenly a familiar sound in Tani's ear.

“Do not let your love for me keep you stuck in one place,” cautioned her grandmother’s voice. “Your journey is happening in two places. One you can see and one you can feel. I will help you this once. But you must keep your eyes open, my little granddaughter. Eyes, heart and mind. Do you understand? Let my love help hold you up. Do not let grief hold you back. And I too must move on. Others will help you in my place. Now listen for the river. Do you hear it? Go toward the river, Granddaughter.”

Tani wiped the tears from her eyes and prepared to move on, toward the faint and distant sound of rushing water. Then just before she took her first step, she thought she saw a face looking out at her from a distant stand of maples. Like the face of an ancient man. Or maybe more like one of the dried apple dolls her grandmother used to make for her. Sparkling black eyes peered out from between the leaves, with skin the color and texture of knotty gray-brown bark. A tall figure with long, thin limbs spotted with patches of greenish lichen, blending perfectly among the straight trunks and branches that surrounded him.

At first Tani was alarmed by the dramatic expression of the craggy face staring back at her. Then feeling a calm understanding deep in her bones she said aloud, “Aha! The Stick Indian. All must be well.” But when she squinted, straining to get a better look, he was gone. So at that Tani took her first step forward, away from her village and past the boundary of the safe and familiar ground she knew so well.

It was not long before Tani found herself at a river’s edge. One of many rivers, creeks and waterways that ran from lake to lake, and on toward the sea. But this river was wide and deep; too treacherous for her to wade across. She stopped and stared to the far bank where she needed to be, frowning at the surface that rushed, swirled and churned before her. The other bank seemed impossibly far. “I am here at the river,” Tani announced to the sky. “And now my path is interrupted. Is it here? Is the heart here on the river bank? I do not see anything but rocks, water, sand and trees.” But her question was met with the rushing hiss of water, a slight breeze against her cheek, and nothing else.

As Tani thought about giving up and turning back, a voice that spoke her language rose up from the gurgling sounds of the river. When she looked down to where the water churned white against fallen logs and big gray rocks, there she saw an otter drifting effortlessly on his back.

"You wish to cross, do you not?" the otter asked.

Tani blinked a few times to see if her eyes were playing tricks on her. But the otter twitched his whiskers, turned his body, and glided back against the current to pass closely in front of her. The thick fur of his belly was dry beneath the sun that shone down upon him. "It is rude not to answer," he said. "You wish to cross the river, do you not? "

Now Tani rubbed her ears, still wondering if she had imagined the words. "Knots and fishhooks!" she exclaimed. "You speak to me in my language."

"You know who I am, of course," said Otter. "And I believe I know who you are."

"I am Tani," she said excitedly. "A little girl on a journey of grave importance. And of course I know who you are."

"You are the little girl heading towards the ocean," said Otter. "I was told of your coming."

"Yes, that is me," Tani replied, nodding her head up and down. "And you are an otter, by golly!"

But the furry animal, still frolicking easily in the strong currents as though it was nothing at all, answered "No, I am not AN otter. I AM Otter."

"I see," said Tani. "Not AN otter. You are THE Otter. Otter in the fur."

"Good. We have that cleared up," Otter replied. "Now I will ask only once more. Do you wish for me to help you to the other side?"

"Why yes," said Tani, her head feeling all wishy-washy. "Absolutely I do!" She was going to ask Otter how it was that he could speak. But when she thought of her grandmother's stories her doubts flapped away like departing birds, up and into the sunny blue sky. Standing there on the shore, speaking to this creature, she felt things were just as they should be. At least for the moment.

"What exactly do you seek on the other side?" asked Otter. "What is out there by the ocean that makes you willing to brave the river and take such a frightening risk?"

"I am searching for the heart of the land," said Tani. "Or the heart of the world. Or was it the heart of the people? Anyway, it is something like that. And I think it must be a stone. Or perhaps a jewel of some kind that one might hang on a necklace. Something so old that it holds a secret power. The answers to...things." Tani did not want to let Otter know she was still very uncertain about this whole affair. But then she admitted, "I guess I am not exactly sure, Otter. I am hoping I will know when I see it."

Otter swam up to the edge and turned sharply so that his thick tail lay on the bank. "Hmmm," was his reply, long whiskers twitching again as he thought this over. "The heart of the world and so on. Well, grab onto my tail and I will help you. Once we enter the current do not let go," he said sternly, "and we will be across before you know it."

At that moment Tani still wondered if this was truly real, or if she was in a dream; back at home fast asleep in her bed next to cousin Droopy Drawers. Then she thought of the Stick Indian and sneaked a glance over her shoulder.

"He is there," said Otter. "But you cannot see him at this moment. He comes and goes. Visible then invisible. A figure with a face, then only a gnarled tree, moving no more than the wind will allow."

"Who is there?" Tani asked.

"The Stick Indian of course," Otter replied, slapping his tail twice against the sand of the bank.

"Can you read my thoughts?" Tani asked in amazement.

"No," Otter replied. "But I understand them. Now, grab hold and let us brave the river." Tani hesitated, eying the icy water; a deep frown on her forehead. But then she decided this adventure was all too important not to take chances, and she climbed down into the water that clutched at her clothing like a hundred strong fingers of icicle.

"Have courage in yourself and faith in me," said Otter. "I will not let you down. And once we are across leave your pain in the water. Let the current wash your heartache far downriver and out to sea. And you will emerge much lighter of heart and spirit. That is the way of your people, is it not?"

"Yes," said Tani. "Something like that. Though I've never needed to do it before." So Tani grabbed onto Otter's tail and they were off; Otter leading them smoothly through the current like a slippery eel. And as he had promised, soon they were across.

Once safely on the far bank, and after Tani had climbed up onto shore, she noticed something strange. Possibly even as strange as the fact that her furry friend was speaking to her. Tani's clothes were already dry. She looked back across the river, and there he was, visible again: a tall, gnarled figure of bark, branches and leaves. But just as her eyes were certain she was truly seeing the Stick Indian, he was gone. And Tani was aware that the sound of the water had become like many voices. Shouts of encouragement, whispers, cautions and murmurings.

"I am so thankful I met you," Tani said to her new friend. "And so happy to know you."

"And I feel the same," said Otter. "A rare interaction indeed. Especially at this time in the world. Travel well, and keep your heart open to the possibilities most humans have grown to ignore. Go forward with a light heart and serious constitution."

"What is a serious constitution?" Tani asked.

Otter wrinkled up his furry face as he considered her question. "Do not let life's hardships slow you down. Your losses are a part of you now. So stack up all of your experiences, one on top of the other, so that you may reach the full height of your character."

Tani considered her reply to this, but Otter had already slipped back into the water and was moving out into the current.

"So much magic," Tani said to the blue sky above her. "So much magic for one day." But of course there would be much, much more.

Tani walked on for many miles and many hours. Now far from the river, the landscape had become thick with blackberry bushes and leafy trees. Human trails gave way to game trails, and the great forest began not far beyond the expanse of maple, madrona and birch trees where Tani plodded along. When she reached a place thick with salmonberry bushes, she stopped and ate many of the ripe orange berries, as the food stores in her pouch were already nearly half-eaten. Now the sun was sinking low in the sky. Not yet all the way down, but lighting up the jagged top edges of the Olympic Mountains with the same beautiful red color that Tani and her grandmother had enjoyed for many evenings on the porch together. But Tani was not thinking about the prettiness of that rosy light on the mountain tops. She was considering the dangers of nightfall; the cold that sneaked its way through the warmest clothing; and how soon she would no longer be able to see where she was going. And here beneath a dense canopy of trees, the ground before her had turned soft and squishy, with countless little creeks and still slews crisscrossing her path in every direction.

By the light of the sun's rays, piercing through the treetops here and there, Tani had been following a narrow deer trail. Sword ferns and horsetails lined the path, with devil's club and thick salmonberry bushes creating a wall of green to either side, their leaves now turning dark and colorless in the failing light. As she stood and watched her path weave through the maze of gloppy mud and underbrush before her, once again Tani felt hope slipping away. The weight of encroaching night and thoughts of braving the dark alone, far from home with no roof above her, made Tani feel small enough to be blown away in the slightest breeze. Although she had walked away from Otter straight-backed and determined, nighttime in the forest was a different matter altogether. And Tani felt afraid. But when she was tempted to turn and find her way home, she once again found that she was not alone.

"Down here," said a voice. "Down here at your feet is where I am."

Tani squinted into the shadows between the brambles and reeds that here came up to her knees, searching for the owner of this new voice.

"The Stick Indian told me of your coming," said the tiny voice that rose up to Tani's ears like the sound of clear water running over little river pebbles. "He was standing next to that very snag just behind you. Right there, only moments ago. He told me you would soon be rounding the corner. And now here you are, nearly stepping on me."

When Tani's eyes adjusted to the darkening shapes and shadows, down at the roots of the underbrush, she realized the words had come from a salamander with a dark brown body that glistened like shiny leather shoes. A great big salamander, two... no, three times bigger than the ones she often found in the woodpile when building a fire for her grandmother's stove.

“Let me guess,” said Tani, feeling suddenly safe and happy at the sight of this creature no longer than her forearm. “You are Salamander.”

“I am in fact a salamander” replied the sweet, good-natured voice from down in the mud. “The humans call us the pacific giant salamander. But my name is Big Ned of the Bog. You may call me Big Ned, or Ned, or Salamander is fine if you prefer.”

“I see,” said Tani. “No room for assuming things out here in the wilds. Have you come to help me?” Tani was polite, but inside she wondered how such a small creature could come to her aid.

“You would never make it through my land alone,” said Big Ned, as if reading her thoughts. “You would wander and become lost. You would sink and become stuck. Without me you would have to turn back. Now follow me closely. But not too close, for in the dark you might step on me. And if I am gone, then you will truly be lost.” So Tani followed, careful not to tread on her new friend, watching his short legs move like maple syrup on pancakes. And as she watched Ned make his way down the path, so small and confident, Tani’s own fear that she herself was not nearly big enough for the task at hand, quickly subsided.

Much time went by, though to Tani it seemed they had travelled only a very short distance. Ned seemed to know this too, for soon he called up to Tani. “Lift me up and place me upon your shoulder. From there I will tell you the direction; where you can step and where you must not.”

Tani obeyed, and in the dark her fingers closed around Salamander’s cold body. She placed him carefully on her shoulder, and when she glanced to the side she could see his throat moving up and down with his heartbeat.

After many turns and changes of direction, Salamander called out, “Just ahead. Just ahead we must stop. Around that thick cluster of cattails. Feel the mud beneath your feet? We are in a place where the mud mixes more with the water. Feel how the earth now gives in. This is the way of the ground in this place. If we go too far you will sink up to your knees. Soon we will reach the great pond with banks that lie far off in every direction. That place is no longer my land. It is the domain of a friend who will take you from there. An expanse of still water with only small islands of firm earth, rising above the surface here and there.”

I am so grateful you are here with me," said Tani. "I am... I mean... I was afraid until I came upon you. I fear I am not very brave, or brave enough for this journey, I should say."

"The brave are not necessarily the ones who go forward feeling no fear," said Salamander. "The brave are more often the ones who go forward even though they are afraid."

"Very smart," said Tani. "Very smart, Little Ned."

"That's Big Ned, the salamander corrected. "And we have arrived."

At the cluster of cattails the two friends stopped. And no sooner had Tani gently placed Salamander back onto the earth than a deep voice greeted the two travelers, like a rumble rising from the opening of a metal bucket. And there on the bank of a great expanse of still water sat an enormous frog. She was as big as Tani, and even heavier. With eyes like softballs on either side of her broad head. And through an opening in the leaves and branches above, the moon shone down, reflecting deep in Frog's eyes, which bulged and glistened like huge black beads of cut glass.

Tani had no time to inquire as to the frog's name, for just as she was about to ask, the frog's voice boomed in a great reverberating belch. "No time to lose," she croaked. "On my back and I will take you over to dry land."

"I am going to ride on your back?" Tani asked, wondering if such an arrangement could possibly work. "Perhaps I should follow you, just as I followed Big Ned?"

"You are clearly a determined child," said Frog. But you must accept my help, for bravery will not get you across these marshes. A capable friend is what you need now."

Tani climbed onto Frog's back. And as she turned to thank Ned for his help and wisdom, Frog took a mighty leap that made Tani's hair blow back, streaming out behind her. She held her breath and prepared to plunge beneath the surface. But just as Salamander had said, there were small islands of solid ground dotting the stagnant surface, and Frog landed perfectly on the first patch of earth that peeked just barely above the water. Frog and Tani touched down for only an instant before they were high into the air once again, as Frog bounced from island to island. Tani was having so much fun on this bumpy ride that she was disappointed when Frog took one final, powerful leap and came to rest safely on the far shore.

"Continue down this deer trail," said Frog. "Straight forward and on into the trees. Soon it will be completely dark, but do not fear the night. There will be others waiting for you." And turning her body around, Frog sprung high into the air, disappearing among the cattails.

"I will watch for the others," Tani called after her. "I will never forget you! And I wish I could repay you for your help!" Tani had wanted to express her sincerest thanks, but Frog was speedily bouncing out of earshot.

“I am off to lay eggs,” Frog’s throaty voice echoed back, already far away in the marshy distance. “Remember me you must. For my tadpoles will need the pure rain and water to live on this earth. You may thank me with your actions. Your actions down the road.”

Tani thought this was a strange thing to say at this particular moment. But inside she promised that she would make a point of remembering Frog’s parting words.

So Tani made her way through a crowded maze of salal bushes, sword ferns and nettles, where mosquitos buzzed about her ears but for some reason did not bite. And soon Tani found herself in a dark place where fir and cedar trees rose up all around. The thick trunks towered skyward in every direction, as far as Tani could see, until the trunks became shadows in the distance, then disappeared altogether within a wall of darkness.

Despite Frog’s encouraging promise of more companions down the trail, the doubt Tani had struggled with became regret as she waited and waited, peering into the domain of night, where shapes and shadows lunged toward her. She grew colder with the complete disappearance of sunlight. But it was not much longer before she heard the next voice.

“Alone in the dark forest,” came a whisper from somewhere above. “Very spooky, is it not? ”

Tani looked up, and as her eyes adjusted she could just make out the sly, whiskered face above her on an overhanging branch. His black and brown mottled fur made him virtually invisible among the cedar boughs. Tani recognized the animal, having seen one only once before, stealing chickens from her grandmother's coup. It was a fisher. A quick and cunning creature, with long sleek body and sharp white teeth.

"You are Fisher," said Tani, more than a little uncomfortable. "Am I right?"

"Yes," Fisher replied, his voice almost a hiss. "Fisher at your service. Are you afraid, little girl? The situation you find yourself in definitely calls for at least a bit of the creepy-crawly nerves."

"Only a little," Tani replied, shivering slightly.

"Very brave," said Fisher. "Such a brave little girl. Out here in the great lonely forest with your very life on the line."

"Oh, don't mind him," came a low growl that made Tani jump. "Sneaky and slippery at the best of times." And when she turned, Tani found herself face to face with the hulking figure of a bear. Her black fur made her shape stand out against the mossy, gray rock wall that sloped up behind her.

"That does not carry much weight, coming from a bear," said Fisher. "Great, toothy beasts, known to eat your kind at the worst of times."

"True," said Bear. "Though I myself have never eaten the flesh of men. Unsavory sounding, I must say. But a Fisher caught napping...well that is something I might consider."

“Well, regardless of sneakiness and eating others,” said Fisher. “Tonight we are your friends.” Then Fisher raised an eyebrow toward Bear. “Friends to you, and friends to each other. Friends who do not consider eating one another up. In fact if we were not your friends, I would have helped myself to that pouch of fish and berries before you even knew I was here.”

Tani’s hand moved to where her small supply of food hung from her belt. “But how did you know...” she began to ask. Then quickly realized who she was talking to. “Of course,” she said. “You probably smelled it from a hundred feet away.”

Fisher twitched his long white whiskers. “Two hundred or more,” he said. “Way back where ‘Ol Froggy bid you farewell.” Then sensing that Tani was not at ease, Fisher added. “Trust that both Bear and I want to see you live. For in the long run little girl, we are stronger when we all survive, regardless of our squabbles in the course of life. Our continued existence together on this earth is what truly matters. Our connection over time is a much stronger thing than the moments when we might consider ourselves enemies.”

At that Tani’s nervousness faded away, knowing she was safe with these two predators of the forest.

“You cannot press on until the first light of morning,” said Bear. “Now you must shelter from the cold. Follow me closely.”

“Yes, here you will spend the night,” said Fisher. “While you sleep I will find a path to the ocean that you can follow. In the morning, with the sun’s light, I will personally guide you there.”

Bear led Tani to a recess in the rock wall behind her, the opening nearly invisible from the thick salal bushes crowding in. “In here,” said Bear, and her great dark body became another shadow as she disappeared inside. Bear just barely fit into the little cave, and Tani curled up against Bear’s warm thick fur. “Dream now, little girl,” said Bear. And in moments, Tani was fast asleep.

And as Bear had told her, Tani did dream. In the dream she found herself speaking to a great audience. She stood in the center of a paved road, newly cut into the old growth forest. And the wild friends Tani had met the day before were all behind her. But in the dream they were not her guides, and they did not have the answers. They stood behind Tani as there was nowhere else for them to go.

“Dear one, it is happening again,” said the same voice she had heard through the window of her uncle’s house. The same voice that had told her it was time to travel. “Bad things are happening in the world.” And when Tani looked around she saw the Stick Indian, closer now than when she had seen him in waking life. “You cannot always stop the things you do not want to happen,” he said to her. “But you will try. And because of who you are, you will often succeed. These times will shape and color the landscape of your life and the lives of others. One of these times is upon you now. Be strong. The future is coming.” Then Tani heard the distant rumble of machines, and her eyes opened to the crisp damp air of early morning deep in the forest; the sun’s rays streaming through the canopy in beams of white light.

When Tani stirred, Bear lifted her head and sniffed the air.

“I had a dream,” said Tani. “I was doing something very important a ways down the road. You were there, and I was somehow protecting you. I know it might sound a little silly, me protecting you.”

“Did you know that the remains of my kind are almost never found by man?” asked Bear, after making some huffing and puffing noises as she thought.

“Why is that?” asked Tani.

“When we know the time is coming soon, when the last sleep can no longer be held at bay, we go deep into the forest. Deep into the brush. To places we believe men will not tread. You have uncles who are hunters, little girl. When you return home, ask them how many times they have found the remains of a bear who has left this world.”

“But why is that?” Tani asked.

Again Bear huffed and puffed softly. “There are places that must not be disturbed. Places that must remain untouched. This is how tomorrow will always be there, when man ensures that the forest is forever, and the wild places remain wild. Otherwise the earth is not as eternal as the old ones believed. You think the notion of you protecting me is silly. But to that I say this. You do not have my gift of physical strength. But you have other gifts which I do not.”

Again Bear sniffed the air, and her ears stood up on her head. “That tough little customer returns,” said Bear. “It is time.”

Tani stretched her arms and legs, looking around for Fisher.

“Up here,” hissed the familiar voice. And there was the cunning fisher, balanced on a cedar bough just above her head. “I have found the way. Not far at all. Soon the sounds of the endless water will be in your ears. Follow me, little girl.”

Tani thanked Bear, who yawned and fell immediately back to sleep. Then she set out after Fisher, who travelled by the trees, jumping and slithering from branch to branch. After a while the trees became sparse, and thick green moss blanketed the ground between their trunks. When Fisher could no longer move from tree to tree, he jumped softly to the ground and trotted down the path in front of Tani. As they walked, Tani ate what would be her last portion of berries and dried fish, making sure she saved half of what was left.

While savoring her last bite, Tani looked up and realized she had lost sight of Fisher. She hurried her step, and when she rounded the last corner there he was perched on a fallen log, looking back at her over his shoulder. And it was at that moment Tani heard the sound of waves rolling against rock and sand. And just beyond Fisher’s silhouette, the sky opened up to a beautiful clear blue expanse with fluffy white clouds floating far out to the horizon.

“The water that cannot be crossed,” said Fisher. “You have made it.”

Tani walked up to Fisher’s side. “Yes, Fisher,” she said. “I am here. But now as I look upon the shore, I am worried that I have made a mistake.”

“And why is that, skinny little child?” asked Fisher, cocking his head to the side.

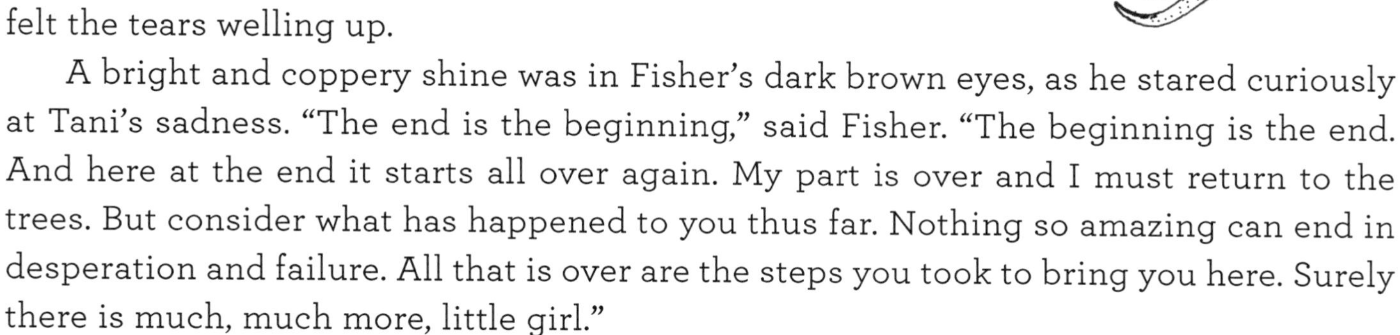

“Because here I am at the end,” Tani replied, shrugging her shoulders and waving her hand towards the shifting tide. “And I have not seen what I have come looking for. What do I do now?” And when Tani revealed her feelings of defeat to Fisher, her voice quavered and she felt the tears welling up.

A bright and coppery shine was in Fisher’s dark brown eyes, as he stared curiously at Tani’s sadness. “The end is the beginning,” said Fisher. “The beginning is the end. And here at the end it starts all over again. My part is over and I must return to the trees. But consider what has happened to you thus far. Nothing so amazing can end in desperation and failure. All that is over are the steps you took to bring you here. Surely there is much, much more, little girl.”

Tani reached down and patted Fisher on the head. “I am so glad you are with me,” she said. “I believe my very life has depended on the animals I have met.”

“And our lives may someday depend on you,” Fisher replied.

Tani then poured the last of her food onto the log next to her chicken-stealing friend. “For you,” she said. “I wish I could give you more.”

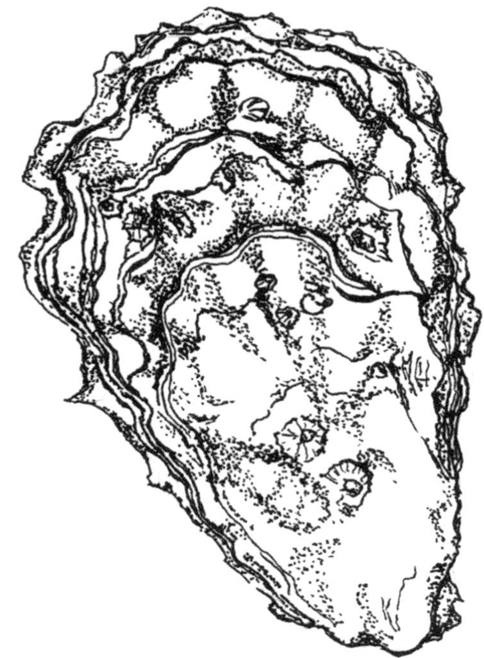

“You see,” said Fisher. “You are far from lost.” And at that he ate the berries and dried fish, thanked Tani, and slinked off into the forest. “If you are hungry there are oysters down there,” he called back. “You gave to me, and now the earth shall give something to you. When the tide is out, the table is set, as they say. The oysters won’t mind. Farewell, little girl.”

“Good idea,” said Tani, remembering the folding knife in her pocket. “I will do that.” Then from somewhere back in the trees Tani faintly heard Fisher’s parting words. “Perhaps I will see you along the trail. Other trails at other times.” And at that Fisher was gone.

Tani walked down to the water's edge, careful not to tread on the patchwork of white shells and barnacles here and there, all along the sandy shore. For now more than ever she was aware of all the life around her, no matter how small. She selected several of the oysters, shucked them with her little knife, and sucked them down. And there she kneeled at the breaking shoreline for what seemed to her to be a very long while, looking out towards the horizon. Despite Fisher's encouragement, she struggled with the notion of what to do next. She even felt anger at herself for not completely understanding her grandmother's words and the task at hand. With all the lessons awakened within her, it appeared there was nowhere else to go. "Surely I cannot be expected to swim out into the waves," Tani said out loud.

But as these words left her mouth, she remembered her grandmother's assurance that she would be shown the way. And since the gifts and guidance of the last days had come true in ways she never would have imagined or believed, then surely there was more to be found. Surely Tani was not at the end. And with this newfound certainty she began walking forward. First up to her ankles. Then further and deeper. Until she felt the surging current lapping at her knees. After a few more steps Tani was waist-deep in the powerful sea. She paused for only a moment. Then dunked down under the dark green water, where eel grass, and kelp beds the color of pea soup, swayed heavily in the swirling tide. And islands of sea foam moved sluggishly with the push and pull of the shifting eddies.

Tani got down on her knees and opened her eyes, cheeks puffed up with air as she held her breath. And there on the sandy bottom, no more than ten feet away, something that appeared to be a grayish stone suddenly flashed bright red, then mellowed into a glowing purplish color.

Tani moved through the water, hope and excitement swelling in her chest as she crawled along the sandy bottom until she was crouched above the stone. "You can stop holding your breath now," said the stone. "Go ahead. Let it go."

"Are you the heart?" Tani exclaimed, air bubbles bursting forth from her mouth; not truly aware of the amazing fact that she was now talking and breathing underwater.

But soon the reddish-purple stone began to move, and eight short legs lined with suction cups unfolded from beneath the little lump. "The heart?" said the creature. "I am Stubby Squid. Stubbiest creature of the sea. And what brings you here, little girl? I take it you are looking for someone named The Heart."

"No, not exactly," said Tani, her words rising to the surface in streams of wobbling bubbles, shining like silvery jewels. "I am looking for the heart of the world. The heart of the people. The heart of all things. Something like that. But here I am at the end of my journey. And surely I cannot be expected to make my way out into the open ocean to search for something I may not even recognize when I see it."

"The end and the beginning. Beginning and the end. As the fur-ball on the beach just told you, it all depends on how you look at things." These words did not come from Stubby Squid. These new voices had come from the deeper water. And when she looked up, Tani saw four little fish swimming toward and around her. The yellow-golden color of their scales became visible as they emerged from the dusky-green of the deep; each of these fishes the size and shape of a ping pong ball.

"More great minds to contribute to solving your mystery," said Stubby Squid.

"And who are you folks?" Tani asked, as the fish swam up to float motionless before her.

"We are pacific spiny lumpsuckers," the four fish replied in unison. "And you are a strange and original sight. What brings you to our world down here beneath the waves?"

"She is searching for the heart of things," Stubby Squid answered on Tani's behalf, rising up on his eight short tentacles. "It seems our home is the only place she has not yet looked."

"Yes," said Tani. "The Heart. But unless the five of you have an idea, I am afraid I have nowhere left to go."

"You are far too smart to draw that conclusion," chimed the choir of lumpsuckers. "The heart of the world. The heart of the people. The heart of all things. Is that not what you said? Why, little girl, have you not yet looked in the most obvious place?"

Tani frowned and began to think. And as her mind journeyed over the steps she had taken so far, her thoughts arrived at the image of her grandmother's hand, holding the moth up before the open window, many weeks ago.

The small and seemingly insignificant insect within the awesome shining circle of the moon. It was the second appearance of the moth that had finally sent Tani on her way. And like the moth beneath the light of a shining star, Tani felt her place among the vastness of life. Never too small to play the most important role.

Suddenly Tani's jaw dropped open and her eyes went wide. "IT IS ME!" She exclaimed.

"There you go," said the lumpsuckers. "It is part of you, and you are part of it. You needed to accept the gifts around you to find the gifts within. No one could simply tell you about something of this importance. You had to seek it out. And coming to understand this truth is likely the destination of your journey."

"And it appears that it has been quite a journey indeed," said Stubby Squid. "But what you sought was there in the great forests. It was on the familiar patch of ground before your front door. It is in the mountains where you may never stand. It is under rocks and stones where you may never look. Everywhere in places both mighty and small. But that does not matter because, yes, the truth of it is carried within you. It is shared with all that surrounds you. And as the lumpsuckers have said, most things of great value are not found without a journey."

"Thank you so much little Stubby and Lumpys!" Tani bubbled. "I see it now! I understand!"

"Your time down here is quickly coming to an end," said Stubby Squid. "You must return to the place of your people, carrying what you have learned."

"But I have more questions," said Tani. "There is so much more!"

But the lumpsuckers were now swimming away, and Tani could barely make out the dots they had become before disappearing completely into the murky depths. And when she looked toward Stubby Squid, she saw that he too was swimming off into the long green stalks of eel grass; his body propelled by nearly invisible fins along his sides, fluttering like angel wings.

"Thank you, little friends," Tani bubbled. And she turned to leave the water.

When Tani broke the surface and blinked the saltwater from her eyes, she gasped at the sight before her. For there, perched on a snag where the beach met the forest was the largest eagle she had ever seen. He opened and closed the glossy brown feathers of his great wings, then turned his head to look straight at her, with piercing eyes that seemed to shine with a light of their own.

"It is time to go home," said Eagle. "Where your kind are waiting for you. Where your people need you. Where we all need you to be."

"Eagle, can you tell me what it is I will be needed for?" Tani asked, afraid she had missed something, despite her overwhelming discoveries.

"Protect and grow the new light within you," said Eagle, "and you will be a light within the darkness of men. People along the path of your life will sometimes let you down. But you must never give up on the lessons of your journey. Your ability to better the world around you; that is what you are needed for."

Tani bowed her head, a sense of pride and purpose warming her to the tips of her fingers and toes.

"Understand this, little girl," said Eagle. "You now have what is needed to move in the direction for which you are destined. Your journey has only just begun."

"I have all I need?" said Tani.

"What you need to continue on," said Eagle. "The understanding of your need to discover even more. The understanding of what it takes to re-awaken what has always been carried within you. Knowledge of places you have already been, but have not yet remembered. And the responsibility of sharing what you find."

"I have been there before. But this time I will go by a road I have never travelled before," said Tani, a film of tears clouding her eyes. "My grandmother told me that."

"She was very wise," said Eagle. "The hand that guided you on those first steps. You were lucky to have one such as her at your beginning. Even though your time with her was shorter than you would have hoped for, your grandmother will always be one of the brightest mornings in all your summers. Alive forever within your heart. And from here, it will be up to you. Now you must learn to speak for those who cannot speak for themselves. Protect those who cannot protect themselves."

As Tani and Eagle rose from the ground, Tani looked down to the beach where she had said goodbye to Fisher. And there just beyond the thickets of the forest edge, down where grass grew up from the open sand, she saw the Stick Indian with one arm raised, his face looking skyward. And in the time it took Tani to blink, there was now only one small tree standing in the spot where the Stick Indian had been; one sapling at the edge of the great forest.

"Will I ever hear your voices again?" asked Tani.

"That is up to you," said Eagle. "It has always been up to you."

On the strength of Eagle's wing beats, the landscape of Tani's journey back was covered very quickly. And soon her village came into view while the sun was still high and bright in the sky. Tani watched the terrain of her homeland change below to the sound of wind rushing through Eagle's feathers. Soon there was the roof of her uncle's house. And standing in the sandy clearing from where Tani had first departed, there she saw the tiny figure of her cousin Droopy Drawers. The little girl raised one chubby arm to wave, as if seeing Tani riding upon the back of an eagle was nothing out of the ordinary. The sight made Tani truly smile for the first time since her grandmother's death. A smile that made her heart swell with happiness and hurt at the same time, as she descended toward the spot where her baby cousin waited, as if she had been expecting Tani to return at that exact moment. A tiny lone figure at the center of an opening in the trees. With the wide world all around her.

Made in the USA
Charleston, SC
03 August 2013